THE RECRUIT

A JACK NOBLE SHORT STORY

L.T. RYAN

LIQUID MIND MEDIA, LLC

THE JACK NOBLE SERIES

Visit http://ltryan.com/noble-intentions/ for purchasing information.

THE RECRUIT

August, 1994: Parris Island, South Carolina

I hovered over the dirt in a push-up position, my face inches from the ground. Parris Island in August is a killer. Eight in the morning and it had to be over ninety degrees. Sweat dripped off my face like a waterfall, turning dirt into mud. My lungs filled with dust and grime every time I sucked wind through my mouth. My muscles burned. Quivered. I thought about standing and squaring off with the scrawny punk who'd spent the last eight weeks trying to break me. But that would result in a nighttime visit from the rest of my platoon. And frankly, I'd grown tired of those.

Drill Instructor Sergeant Kaszlaski wove a tapestry of obscenities from above me. "Maggot Noble, you sonovabitch. Don't you dare touch the friggin ground." He kicked me in the ribs. "This is why maggots like you don't belong in my Marine Corps."

I said nothing. Held firm and remained still.

He placed his boot in the middle of my back. I pictured him, one knee raised, leaning over, arm crossed over his thigh. Some kind of victory pose. He leaned in, trying to use his weight to force my

1

stomach to the ground. The entire platoon shouted from the human barrier they created, encircling me and the good Sergeant. Their shouts of encouragement, or threats, kept me stiff and unbending. God forbid I touch the ground. We'd all be in the shit if I did.

"C'mon, Noble," Riley "Bear" Logan's deep voice rumbled from behind me. Bear already had me on his "hit to kill" list. If the platoon got in any more trouble on my account, he'd be sure to visit me in the middle of the night. Given the choice of the platoon or Bear visiting, I'd take the platoon. The guy was massive.

The boot lifted. I reacted by arching my back, loosening my core muscles.

"What the hell was that, shitbag." Kaszlaski dropped to the ground. Stuck his face next to mine. "Did you just lift up? Did I see you lift your back up?" Spittle sprayed across my face and shaved head. His hot breath felt swampy against my sweat covered head. "Holy shit, Noble. Do you know what this means?"

The platoon let out a collective groan. I didn't need to look up to feel their eyes burning a hole in my back. The entire group would pay for my perceived failure.

"Damn you, maggot," Kaszlaski said. "Get the frig off the ground."

I didn't move.

Kaszlaski changed my mind with a well-placed kick to the side of my head. My vision flashed as his dust covered black combat boot landed next to my temple. I collapsed into a pile on the ground. My sweat absorbed the dirt and I felt it form a cake-like coating on my cheek and forehead. I questioned my decision to join the Marine Corps as the side of my head thumped with pain. I could be in California right now, preparing for my freshman season as quarterback at one of the top college programs in the nation.

"Get to the barracks, recruits" Kaszlaski said. "We've got something special prepared for all of you this afternoon." He stood a few feet away from me.

I had to get up before it was just me and him out here. I tried to push my body up. Fell back on my face. I rolled over, wiped my face with my sleeve and looked up at the cloudy sky. Thunder rumbled in the distance. That, or the kick to my head was harder than I realized.

I blinked and saw Bear standing over me. His large frame blocked the dull glow of the sun from behind the clouds. "Whatever he makes us do, you're getting triple from me."

I smiled.

Bear didn't. He spat on the ground, turned and walked away.

Kaszlaski stood over me. "Get the frig up, maggot."

We stood in front of our racks. Two straight lines of recruits, facing each other. All of us at attention, arms behind our backs, dressed in our physical training uniforms. No one said a word. I looked down the line opposite me. No one made eye contact.

Kaszlaski and two other drill instructors entered the room. The sound of shuffling filled the room as each recruit straightened up in preparation of the D.I.s punishment.

"Recruits," Kaszlaski said. "Despite Maggot Noble's miserable failings at keeping himself off of the ground," he stopped in front of me and smiled without looking at me, "we have a treat for you today." He continued walking while saying nothing.

No one said anything.

"Today we are going to pay a visit to the boxing ring," he continued. "Because nothing gives me more pleasure than seeing my recruits pounding the crap out of each other. This is the moment in recruit training that you should live for. And if you don't you just need to get the hell out of my barracks." He stopped and looked around as if waiting for half the platoon to leave. "It's where one maggot will redefine himself and become slightly greater that worth-

3

less to me. And one or two of you will find yourself even lower than maggot on my totem pole."

I felt every eye in the room focus on me. I glanced around to confirm my suspicion. Big mistake.

"God dammit, maggot Noble." Kaszlaski spun on his heel and stopped in front of me. "Step forward."

I took a single step forward.

"This worthless recruit standing in front of me is going fight first," he said. "What do you think of that, recruit?"

"This recruit is happy to fight first, Drill Instructor Sergeant Kaszlaski, Sir." I hated saying that and infused every ounce of sarcastic tone I could muster.

He inched closer to my face, smiled and exhaled heavily. The smell of corn chips invaded my nose. I kept my eyes straight ahead, staring into dead space. He shifted and bobbed his head in front of mine, trying to catch my eye. Any excuse to plant a fist in my gut. I refused to fall for it. Picked a point on the drab cream colored wall and kept my eyes fixed on it.

"Who then," he spun on his heel, "should we get to fight you?" He walked to the far end of the room. "Do I have any recruits who are willing to take on maggot Noble in the first match?"

The room remained silent.

"Holy crap," he said while continuing to pace the room. "Am I to believe that Maggot Noble is so popular no one wants to fight with him? Recruit Noble, did you know you were so popular?"

I didn't answer.

"Or is it that you recruits are scared to fight him?"

The room stayed silent.

"If a recruit doesn't step up now you'll, all of you shitbags will have to deal with me." He stopped in front of Bear.

Bear stepped forward. "This recruit will fight in the first match, Drill Instructor Sergeant Kaszlaski, Sir."

"Well now, here's a recruit who might actually make something of himself," Kaszlaski said. "Are you telling me that you're volunteering for the first fight, recruit Logan?"

"This recruit wants nothing more than to take place in the first fight against recruit Noble, Drill Instructor Sergeant Kaszlaski, Sir."

I turned my head. This time Bear turned and met my stare.

He smiled.

I didn't.

***

Kaszlaski and the other D.I.s led us outside, behind the barracks. Bear walked next to Kaszlaski. The other two D.I.s guided me through the light rain by my elbows.

"Round up," Kaszlaski said.

The platoon formed a loose circle, pushing me toward the middle. Bear stood across from me. Massive didn't begin to describe him. He shrugged his shoulders and swung his head side to side. He kept his eyes focused on me the entire time. The three D.I.s surrounded him, slapping at his chest and yelling at him.

I turned, looking for support. One of the other recruits spit at me. Another taunted me to come at him. This was a no win situation if I'd ever been in one. I turned back around. The reaction from the platoon was a mixture of cheering for Bear and cursing at me.

Kaszlaski moved to the center of the makeshift ring. He motioned at Bear and I to meet in the middle.

"I want a fight," he said. "It don't have to be clean." A smile swept across his face as he winked at Bear. "Touch hands."

Our ungloved fists bumped together inside the empty space between us.

"Fight," Kaszlaski said.

I brought my hands up in a defensive position. Out of the corner of my eye I saw Kaszlaski twist. I didn't see it fast enough, though. He delivered a blow to my back, just below my ribs. Pain ripped through my side. I bent over and turned away. I knew I had to get my bearings and locate Bear. I swung my head around in time to connect with a right hook thrown by the big man. The force of the blow spun me and I fell to the ground. I went unconscious for a moment, but the cold rain drops snapped me back to reality.

The human circle erupted. The platoon cheered the cheap shot and subsequent death blow by Bear.

I got to my knees and crawled to the edge of the pit. I heard Kaszlaski's counting in the background. The sound of it echoed in my head.

"Just stay down, maggot," he said.

The line of recruits separated as I neared them, giving way to the stacked cinder block wall that made up the barracks. I pressed against the wall and got to my feet. Turned. Focused my eyes on Bear. "That all you got?"

Bear smiled. Charged at me. I took a step forward, then slipped to the side as he lifted his hand over his shoulder and swung at me. He crashed into the wall. A normal man would have collapsed at the impact. It just seemed to piss Bear off.

I backed up to the other side of the ring, staying out of reach of the recruits and keeping Kaszlaski a good distance away.

Bear came at me again, the smile gone from his face.

I waited again. Took a step forward, then slipped to the side, sending him reeling into a group of recruits. They managed to stop his momentum and turn him around.

"Fight me," he said.

I shrugged. Walked to the middle of the ring.

Bear met me there. No one could accuse me of being a small guy, but Bear towered over me. He started throwing short armed jabs. I ducked, circling around him. It was tricky to maneuver in the pit. The footing was unsure and there was always the risk that Kaszlaski was close by and might sucker punch me again. Finally, Bear managed to land a punch on me. The force of it drove me back a few feet.

The platoon erupted in approval again.

The smile returned to Bear's face. "Now I finish this," he said.

I winked.

It threw him off. His eyes narrowed and his smiled faded. His stance opened slightly.

I didn't hesitate. I twisted, launched myself into the air, and brought my fist down across the bridge of his nose, right between his eyes.

Bear staggered backwards. His arms swung blindly, cutting through the air.

I ducked his blows, came up between his outstretched arms and delivered an uppercut to his jaw.

He fell back against a group of recruits. They pushed him forward. He fell to his knees before collapsing on the muddy ground.

The platoon went silent.

Kaszlaski and the other two drill instructors moved into the circle and stood across from me. I braced myself for the attack. Instead, they turned their attention to Bear and helped him off the ground. The recruit circle parted as two D.I.s helped Bear back to the barracks, his big arms draped around their shoulders.

Kaszlaski addressed the platoon. "Everyone back to the barracks. No more boxing today." He stood firm, eyes locked on mine, while the platoon filed through the small path between two sets of barracks.

The rain fell hard and the wind whipped, driving spears of rain into my face. I struggled to keep my eyes open against the onslaught.

"I'll deal with you later, recruit Noble."

That night I lay on my rack, hands clasped behind my head

staring up at nothing in particular. None of the other recruits had said a word to me. A few looked at me, rage burning in their eyes. Bear and a few others gathered at the far end of the room. I overheard them mention my name and something about revenge tonight. I expected it. I was prepared for it.

Kaszlaski stepped in to the room. "Lights out, recruits."

Everyone settled in and the room fell quiet. Minutes passed, then hours. Just as I started to doze off I heard a noise. I braced myself for the attack, but it never came. Instead, I heard whispers. I turned my head slowly toward the voices. Three men stood over Bear's rack. I couldn't make out what they were saying, but a minute later Bear got up and left the men.

I waited a beat, got up and made my way to the door.

"Noble, get the frig back in bed," Hardwood said. He was the old man in the group at age twenty-six. We called him Pops. He'd been the only friend I'd made after eight weeks in this hell hole.

"Going to the head, Pops" I said.

"Hurry the hell up, Noble."

I walked toward the head, turned to the right and stopped in front of the door leading outside. I put my ear to the door. Heard nothing. Inside, the room remained still. Quiet. No one was up, except for maybe Hardwood, but I had no reason to worry about him. I grabbed the handle and turned it, slow and easy. Pulled the door open wide enough to squeeze my body through. I shut the door, keeping the handle turned until completely shut so the latch wouldn't make any noise.

It had cooled off to a sweltering and humid eighty degrees. The thick air created an instant layer of sweat that covered my body. I looked up. The clouds had disappeared. A thin sliver of the moon provided no light. To my right, artificial post lights lit up the end of the barracks. I pressed my back to the wall and moved to the left, where it was dark. Every few feet I stopped and listened. As I neared the corner I heard voices. Too far away to make out, though.

I rounded the corner and moved toward the back of the building. Stopped at the end of the wall. Listened.

"I can't believe you, Logan," Kaszlaski said. "Here we give you the chance to beat the shit out of Noble, and you let him kick your ass."

Bear said, "I didn't know—"

"Didn't know you couldn't fight?" Kaszlaski said.

Bear said nothing.

"What are you, six foot six?" Kaszlaski said. "I didn't know they made pussies that big. Holy shit, Logan."

"I didn't think he was going to come back from that first hit the way he did," Bear said. "Just give me another chance to—"

I heard a slapping sound. Peeked around the corner and saw Bear standing with his back to the building. Kaszlaski stood in front of him, arm outstretched, inches from Bear's face. The big man stood there, mouth open, shoulders slumped. I didn't know if he was going to try to kill Kaszlaski for slapping him or cry about it.

"Don't you ever touch me again," Bear said.

"Or what?" Kaszlaski looked back at the other D.I.'s. They laughed. He twisted his body fast and whipped an open hand across Bear's face.

Bear's head snapped back. When it returned to its normal position he said, "I warned you not to do that."

Kaszlaski squared up and leaned in toward Bear, dwarfed by the massive man. "What are you gonna do about it?"

Bear said nothing.

"That's what I thought." Kaszlaski punched him in the stomach.

This time Bear reacted. He stepped forward and brought both his arms up, driving them through the drill instructor's torso, lifting him off the ground. Bear tossed him at least six feet through the air. Kaszlaski hit the ground with a thud.

The two other D.I.'s lunged at Bear. They fought to restrain him, one on his back, the other at his side. Kaszlaski got to his feet. Pulled something from his pocket. I squinted and leaned in to get a better look. He moved toward Bear and swung his arm. The object in his hand crashed against Bear's head with a thud.

The big man's knees gave out a bit and he dropped a few inches. The two D.I.s held him up.

"Look at the big bad Bear now," Kaszlaski said. "Look at me, maggot."

Bear lifted his head.

"The way this will go down," he swung the object again hitting Bear in the midsection, "is that your platoon turned on you after your pussy showing this afternoon."

The D.I.'s let go of Bear. He fell to his knees. He kept his body straight and his head up.

"My suggestion," Kaszlaski paused and pointed at the other D.I.'s, "our suggestion, is that you should be rolled back."

Bear brought one leg up and started to move the other.

Kaszlaski responded by driving the object over Bear's head again.

I stepped out from behind the wall. "Enough."

The three D.I.s turned to face me. Bear's head swung to the side. No one said anything.

"Leave him alone, Kaszlaski," I said.

"What the hell did you just call me, Noble?"

"You heard me."

Kaszlaski held his position. The other two D.I.s started moving out to surround me. One slipped past my peripheral vision and the other stopped at the edge of it.

"You don't want to do this," I said, moving a few feet away from the wall.

"This is even better," Kaszlaski said, his face breaking into a smile. "You see, we found the two of you," he pointed at Bear and I, "outside fighting. You wouldn't stop. So we had to get involved, and once we did, you two started swinging at us. We had no choice but to fight back."

I said nothing. Didn't move.

"Yeah, now you're not getting rolled. You're getting court

martialed." He looked toward the other two D.I.s. "Hit each other a couple times. Make it look like we got into it with them."

Bear quietly got to his feet. Looked over at me. Nodded.

Kaszlaski must have spotted my slight nod back. He swung his arm and caught Bear on the side of the head. Followed it up with a blow of his fist.

The other D.I.s were busy trading blows to make it look like we attacked them.

I decided to make my move. I moved toward Kaszlaski. He squared up to face me, his arm drawn back, waiting to swing at me with the weapon clutched tightly in his hand. I led with my head and waited for him to bring his arm down. I ducked, slipped to the side, and came up next to him. Delivered a blow to his back, just under his ribs. His body twisted and he dropped his weapon. I grabbed the back of his head and slammed my knee into his face.

Kaszlaski grunted and went limp.

The other two D.I.s stopped trading blows and ran over.

I glanced at Bear. He struggled to get to his feet.

The D.I.s split up. One headed toward Bear. I tried to land a blow on him, but the second D.I. tackled me. We hit the ground hard with him ending up on my back. I felt my head and neck pulled back as he wrapped his arm around me in a choke hold. I watched as the other D.I. stood over Bear, kicking him in the chest and head. The big man swayed on his knees.

I reached up and found the face of my attacker, pressing my thumb into his eye. It didn't take long for his grip on my neck to loosen and I managed to swing him over my shoulder. I scrambled to my feet and lunged at the man standing over Bear. My shoulder connected with his midsection and I lifted him into the air and then slammed him into the ground. A few feet away I spotted the weapon Kaszlaski had used on Bear. A black, hard rubber sap, or blackjack as it is more commonly referred to. I scooped it up and got to my feet, my back against the concrete wall of the barracks.

Bear used the wall to get to his feet. Blood ran down his face from an open wound on his forehead.

Kaszlaski and the other two drill instructors grouped up.

We faced off like gunmen at the OK Corral.

I looked over at Bear. He turned and met my stare. A wicked smile crept across his face and he nodded.

Kaszlaski and the D.I. to his left moved toward Bear. The other D.I. came toward me. I charged Kaszlaski and swung the sap, hitting him in the abdomen. He dropped to the ground in a ball. His buddies followed suit quickly. We stood over their limp bodies like triumphant gladiators.

I turned to Bear. "You OK?"

He nodded. "Sorry, Jack. I misjudged you."

I shrugged. Said nothing.

"You had nothing to gain by helping me out here." He held out his hand. "I got your back now."

I shook his hand, nodded. "We should get inside." I started to toward the stretch of grass between the barracks. "Got a feeling we're going to be visited very soon."

We cleaned up and sat on Bear's rack, waiting in silence for the MPs to arrive. It took longer than I expected, but once they entered the barracks, it went exactly as I expected.

"Noble, Logan," a voice called from outside the barracks. "On your feet."

We stood in the empty space between the two long rows of racks where our platoon slept. The lights flicked on. Groans erupted throughout the room. By this point in recruit training, we were well aware of how long our seven hours of nightly sleep lasted.

The MPs entered, handcuffed us, and led us out of the barracks.

We were marched across base. Four in the morning and it was shaping up to be another scorcher. The air was still and thick. My bound arms prevented me from wiping the sweat from my brow. It ran down my face and burned the cuts and scrapes from the two fights. I looked up at the sliver of moonlight light penetrating through silver clouds.

"Stop here, recruits," the lead MP said.

We stopped. I looked over at Bear. He shook his head.

The MP walked out of earshot with his handheld radio.

"What you think they're gonna do with us?" Bear asked.

I shrugged. "Promotion?"

Bear laughed. "Stop messing around. We're in deep shit, Jack."

"Guess we'll find out." I nodded toward the MP walking toward us.

"Let's go, recruits."

We continued and stopped in front of the main administrative building. It looked dark and deserted from the outside. The MP led us into the lobby. Another MP met us halfway, led us to an interior set of doors and unlocked them.

"What's back here?" Bear said.

I shook my head. I had no clue.

They led us through a maze of halls. We stopped in front of a glass walled office. On the door was a sign that said *Brig. Gen. Keller, Parris Island's Commanding Officer.*

"Sit," the MP said.

We sat on a bench, arms cuffed behind us, and waited.

"We're in deep shit, Bear," I said.

He laughed.

"Shut up, recruits," the MP said. The short bastard had the gumption to place his hand on his pistol as he said it.

I sat back. Sighed. Looked down the hall and at the office across from us, but there wasn't much to see.

Lights flickered on and footsteps echoed through the hall.

Brig. Gen. Keller appeared. He glanced at me, then Bear, then lifted his eyes up toward the MP. "See them to my office." He turned and walked past us.

"Get up," the MP said.

We stood and he let us into the office. He unlocked the handcuffs and removed them from our wrists. "Sit."

We did.

He waited in the doorway.

"That'll be all, Corporal." The glass door shut and Brig. Gen. Keller took his seat across from us.

It sounded like Bear had stopped breathing. I looked over at him. Sweat covered his wide face, which had turned red.

Keller looked down at the papers on his desk, sighed, and looked up at us. "Recruits," he snatched the papers up and straightened them out by tapping them against the desk, "what the hell happened tonight?"

I sat up straight. "Sir, we—"

"Shut up, Noble," he said. "Am I to believe that the two of you got up in the middle of the night, left your barracks, went behind the building and started fighting?"

We said nothing.

He stared at us for a moment, then reached into this pocket and pulled out a pack of cigarettes. "Smoke?"

We both nodded.

He lit three cigarettes, handed one to each of us, then took a long draw on his. He exhaled and sipped on his coffee. "Did either of you need coffee?"

Bear nodded.

"Yes, Sir," I said.

"Corporal," Keller said.

The MP opened the door.

"Get these two some coffee." He turned his attention back to us. "Kaszlaski's a piece of shit." He paused. Pointed at us. "Don't quote me on that. But he is. He blamed this whole thing on you, Noble."

"Sir, with all due respect," I said. "He's a friggin liar."

14

Keller shook his head. "I know." He leaned back in his chair. Took a long drag on his cigarette. "I served with your father and uncle, Jack. Know what kind of men they were. Know the kind of man your dad raised you to be."

I nodded. Said nothing.

"The news of your uncle's death hit me pretty hard," Keller said.

"Me too, Sir."

Keller smiled at me. "Was excited when I saw your name on the recruit list. Been watching over you, so to speak."

"How so?" I said.

He continued without acknowledging my question. "Probably why Kaszlaski hated you so much. He certainly wasn't doing it to make you a better Marine."

"What's this got to do with me then?" Bear asked.

"You just got in the way," Keller said. "He must have figured of all the recruits, you were the one who could beat Jack down. He might have been right. He just didn't know enough about Jack."

Keller winked.

I smiled.

"Got that right," Bear said, rubbing his forehead.

A knock at the door startled jarred three of us. The MP stepped in and placed two cups of coffee on the desk.

Keller nodded at him and waited for the door to close. "I've got a problem now." He leaned forward, placed his elbows on the desk and steepled his hands together. "I've got to figure out how to solve this problem without sending you two to court martial and without pissing off my D.I.s. No matter what I say, most of them will believe Kaszlaski."

"So you know what happened tonight?" I said.

"Yeah," Keller said. "They attacked Bear. You stepped in to help him. Then the two of you kicked their asses."

The room fell silent, save for the occasional sips of coffee. Keller lit three more cigarettes. Handed one to each of us and then turned his attention back to the papers on his desk.

"Does that have anything to do with us?" I asked.

He nodded, his cigarette dangling from his mouth. The smoke wrapped around his head on its way to the ceiling.

"What is it?" I asked.

"I don't want to roll you guys back. You're halfway through recruit training," he paused, his fingers working against pronounced jaw muscles. "Makes no sense to put you through this again. You're ready."

I leaned forward. "Sir, are you saying—"

He waved me off. "But I can't just graduate you. Not with this group, at least."

"The papers?" Bear said.

"Yes, the papers. Someone wants me to loan them a couple of my Marines. Only, they don't want Marines, not true Devil Dogs. They want a couple of promising recruits." He shook his head. "Apparently they want to take what I've begun molding and shape it to what they want." He grimaced and looked to the side.

I looked at Bear. His eyes narrowed as he soaked in Keller's words.

"Who is it?" I asked. "Who wants us?"

"Can't say," Keller said.

"Why not?" Bear asked.

"I've had my eye on you for this, Jack. Since you arrived." He looked at Bear. "Turns out I have your perfect partner now."

I sat back in my chair and interlaced my fingers behind my head. Took in a deep breath and exhaled. "Don't we have a say in this?"

Keller looked at me. Cleared his throat as he fidgeted with the papers. "No."

"Just tell me who it is," I said.

"You'll find out soon enough."

"NSA?"

Keller said nothing.

"DEA?"

He chuckled.

"CIA?"

He cleared his throat. "Lt. Col. Abbot heads up our side of the operation. You two are leaving at oh six hundred hours. You'll be taken to Virginia, where you'll be briefed by him and then begin your training."

"Langley?" I asked.

"I honestly don't know, Noble."

I turned to Bear. "What you think? Partners?"

"Works for me," Bear said.

"We're good to go, General."

THE END

Visit http://ltryan.com/noble-intentions for more information on the Jack Noble Series.

ALSO BY L.T. RYAN

Jack Noble Series

The Recruit

Noble Beginnings

A Deadly Distance

Ripple Effect (Bear & Noble)

Thin Line

Noble Intentions

When Dead in Greece

Noble Retribution

Noble Betrayal

Never Go Home

Beyond Betrayal (Clarissa Abbot)

Noble Judgment

Never Cry Mercy

Deadline

End Game

Mitch Tanner Series

The Depth of Darkness

Into the Darkness

Deliver Us From Darkness (Summer, 2018)

Made in United States
Orlando, FL
29 April 2024

46315528R00017